TANA HOBAN

LOOK! LOOK! LOOK!

Greenwillow Books New York

The photographs were
reproduced from 35-mm slides
and printed in full color.

Greenwillow Books,
a division of William
Morrow & Company, Inc.,
1350 Avenue of the Americas,
New York, NY 10019.
Printed in Singapore
by Tien Wah Press
First Edition
10 9 8 7 6 5 4 3 2

Library of Congress
Cataloging in Publication Data
Hoban, Tana.
Look! look! look! / by Tana Hoban.
p.   cm.
Summary:
Photographs of familiar
objects are first viewed
through a cut-out hole,
then in their entirety.
ISBN 0-688-07239-9.
ISBN 0-688-07240-2 (lib. bdg.)
[1. Visual perception.
2. Toy and movable books.
3. Picture books.]
I. Title.
PZ7.H638Lo 1988
[E]—dc19
87-25655   CIP   AC

THIS ONE IS FOR
VIVIAN ROSENBERG

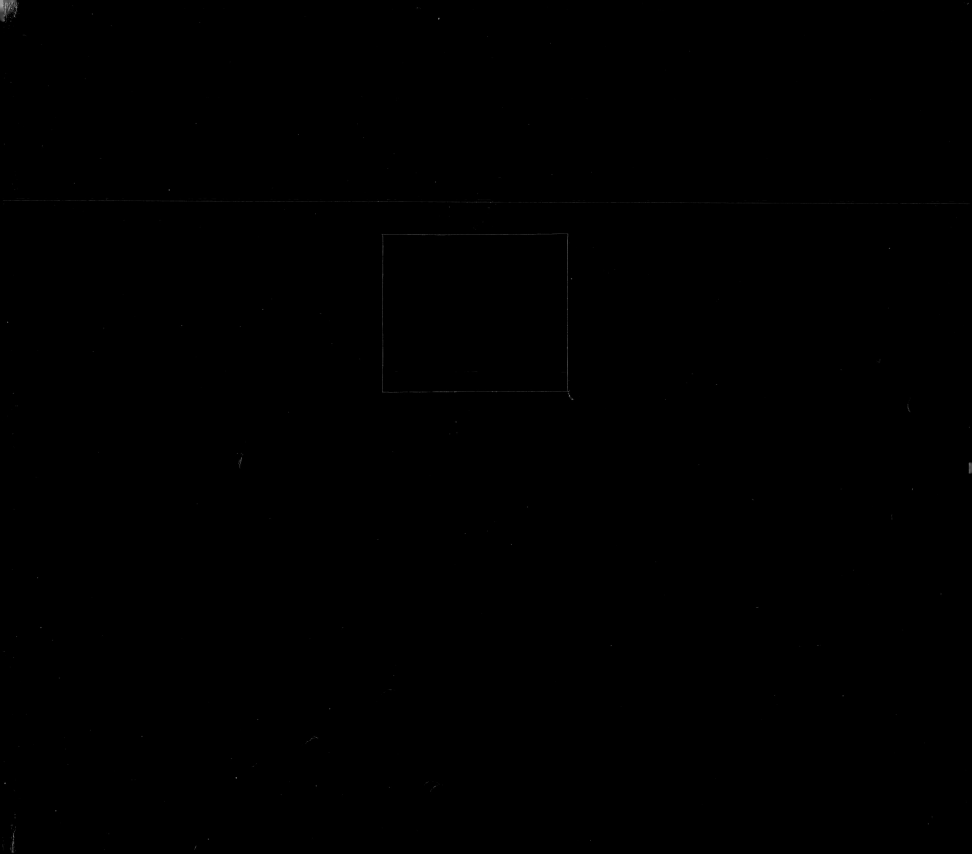

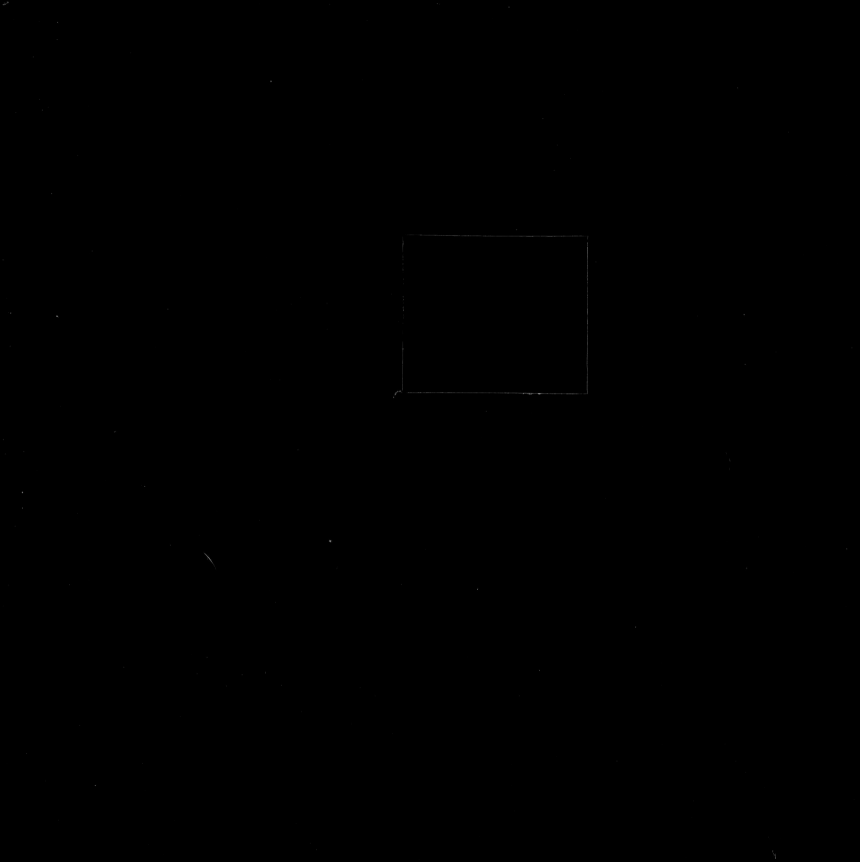

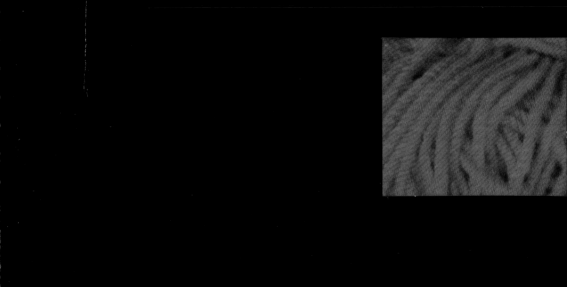

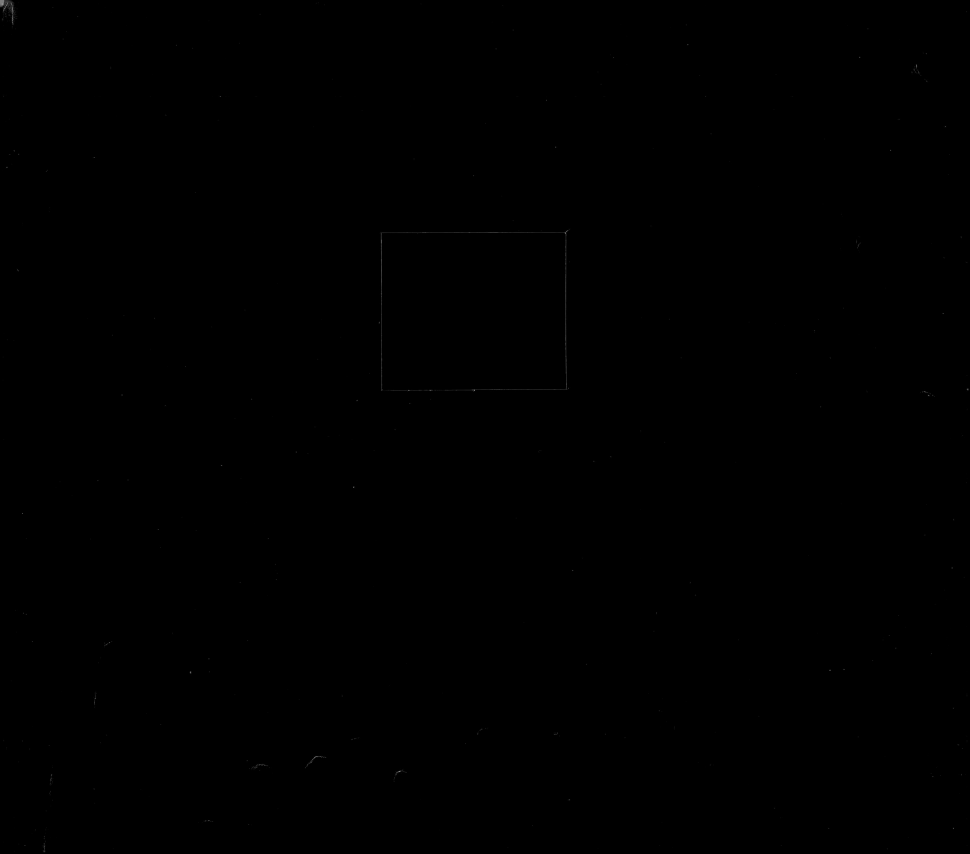

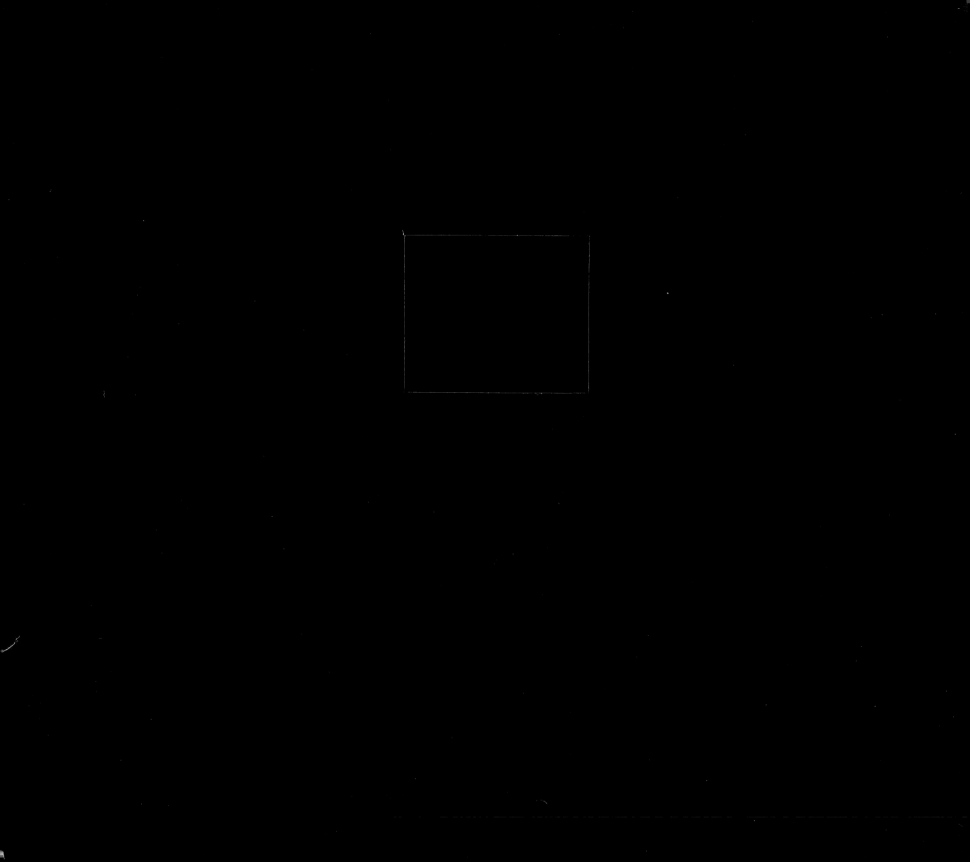

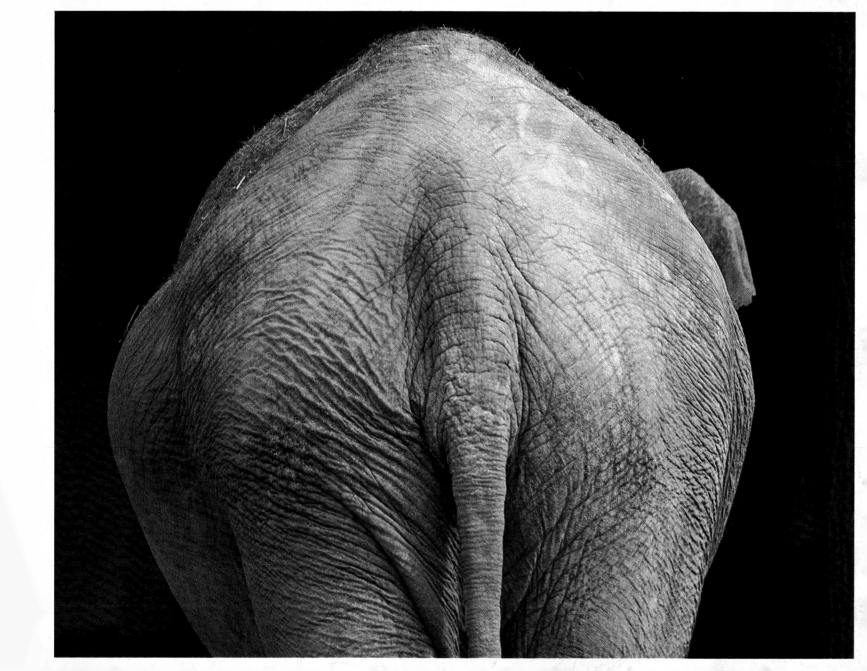

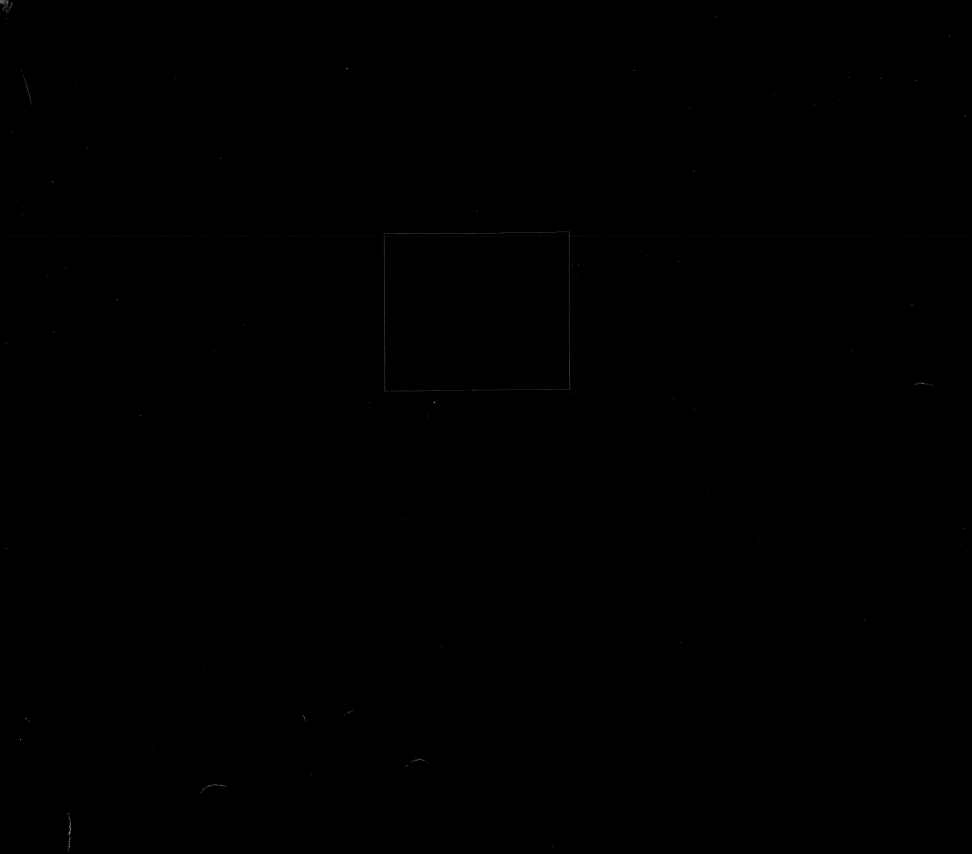

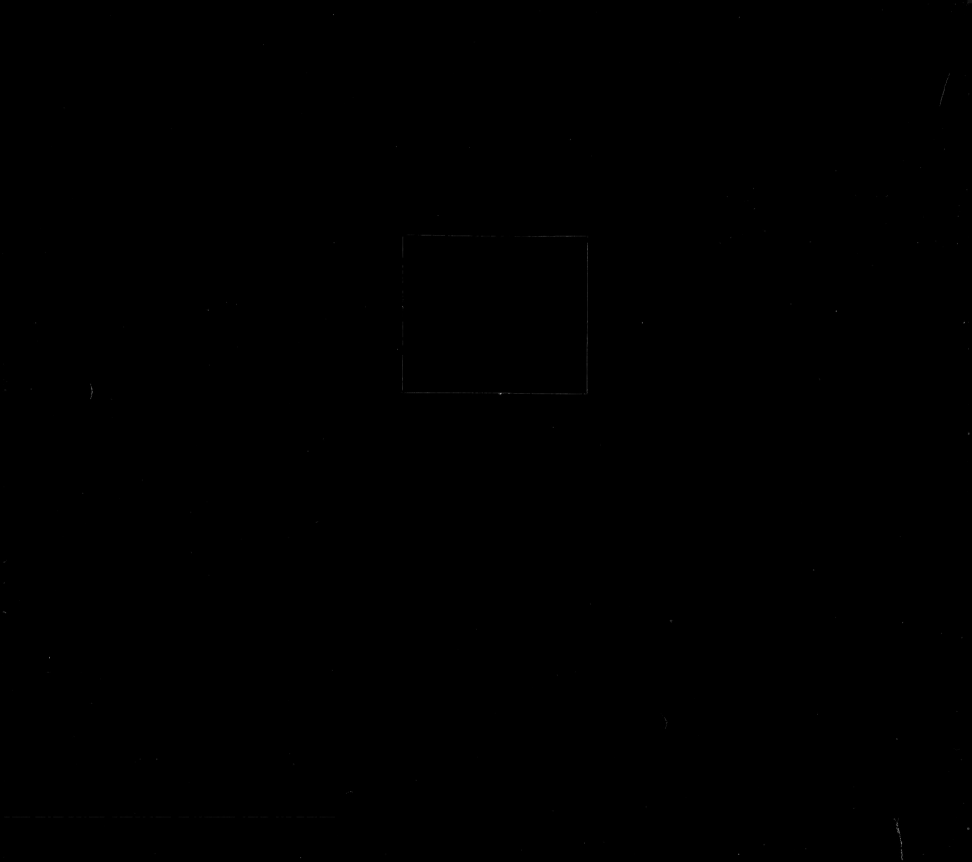

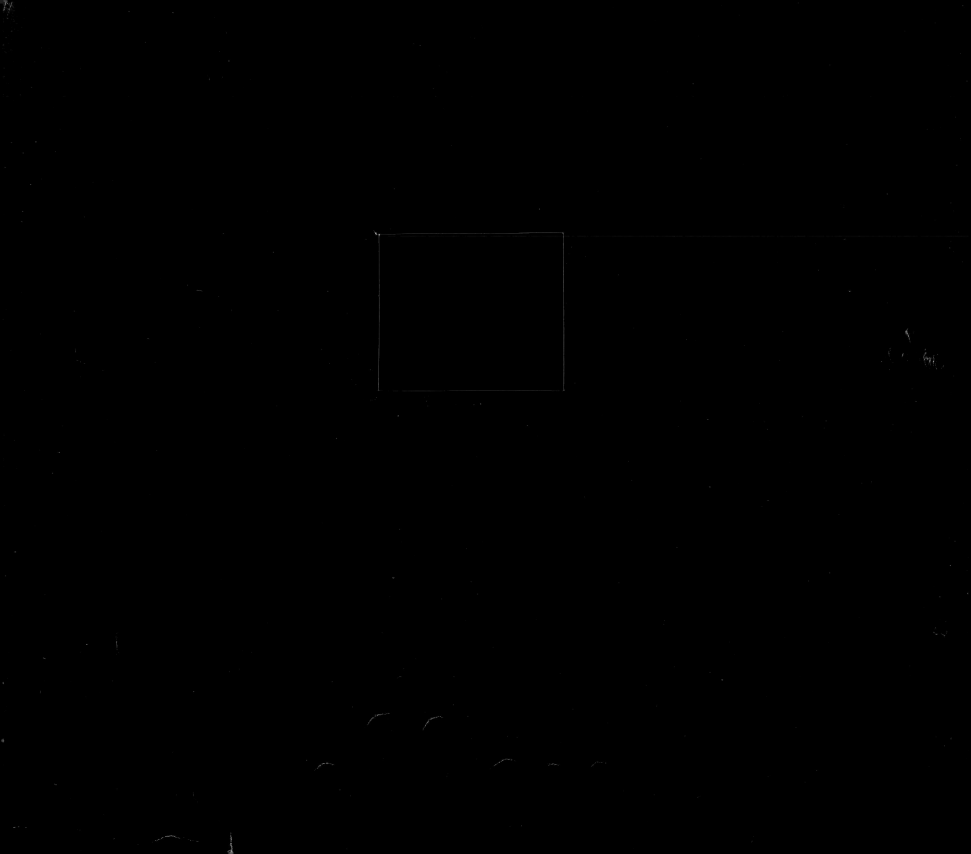

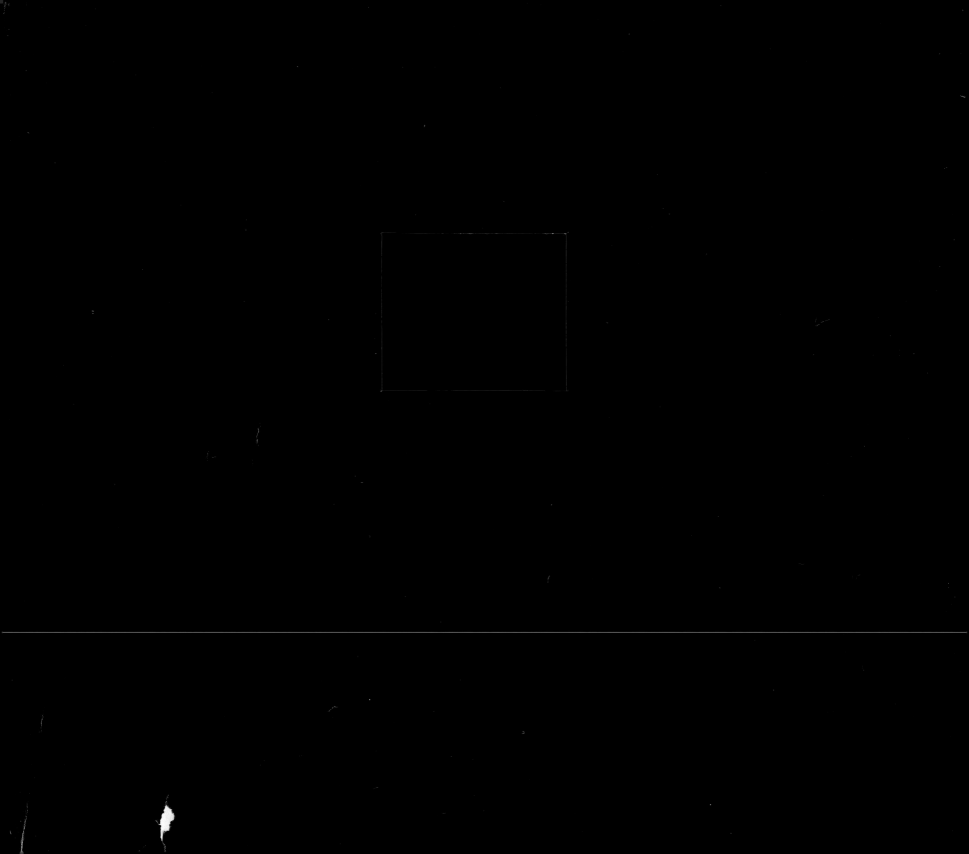

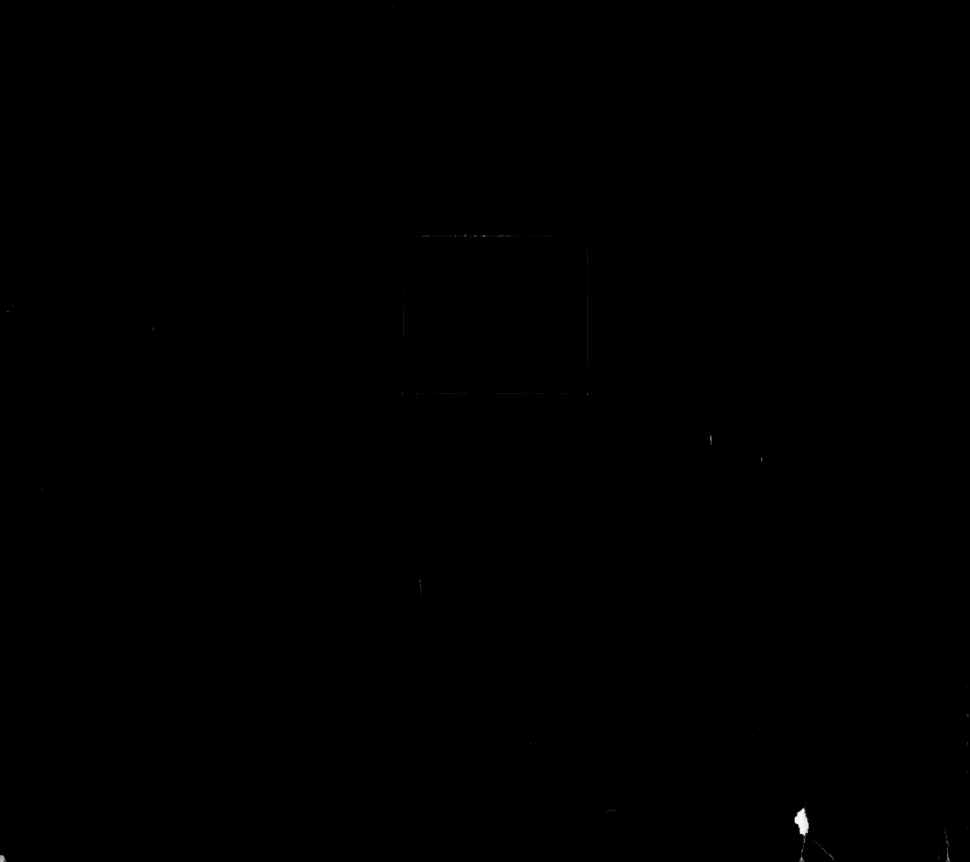

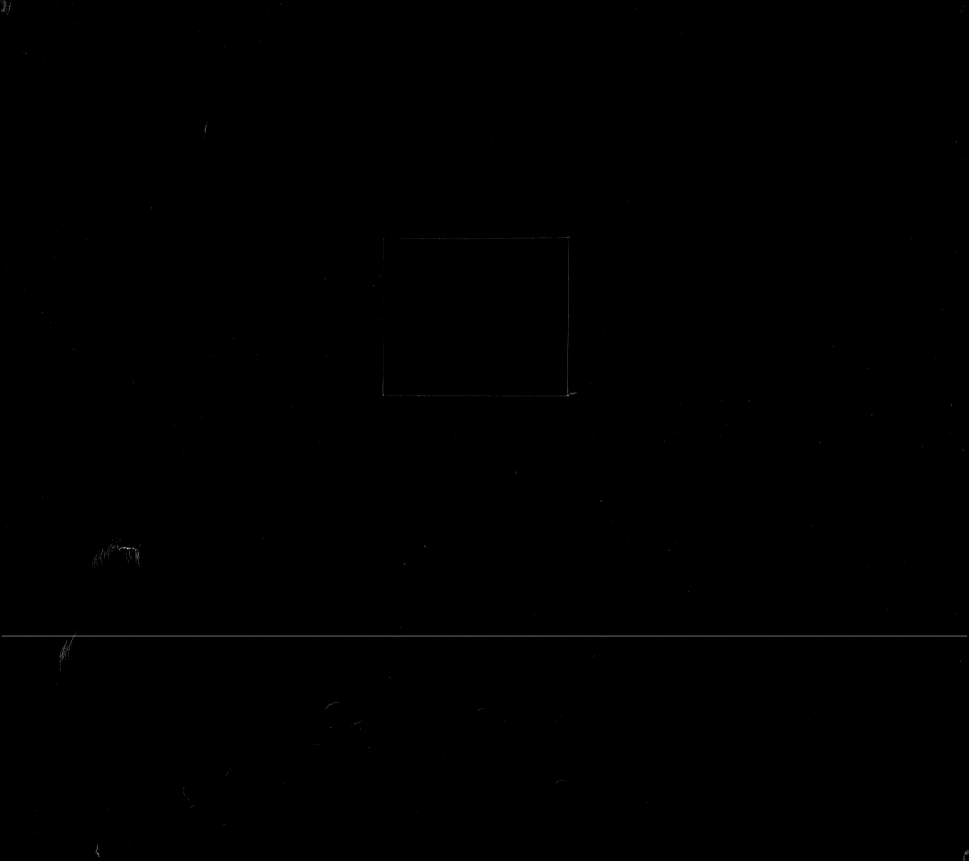

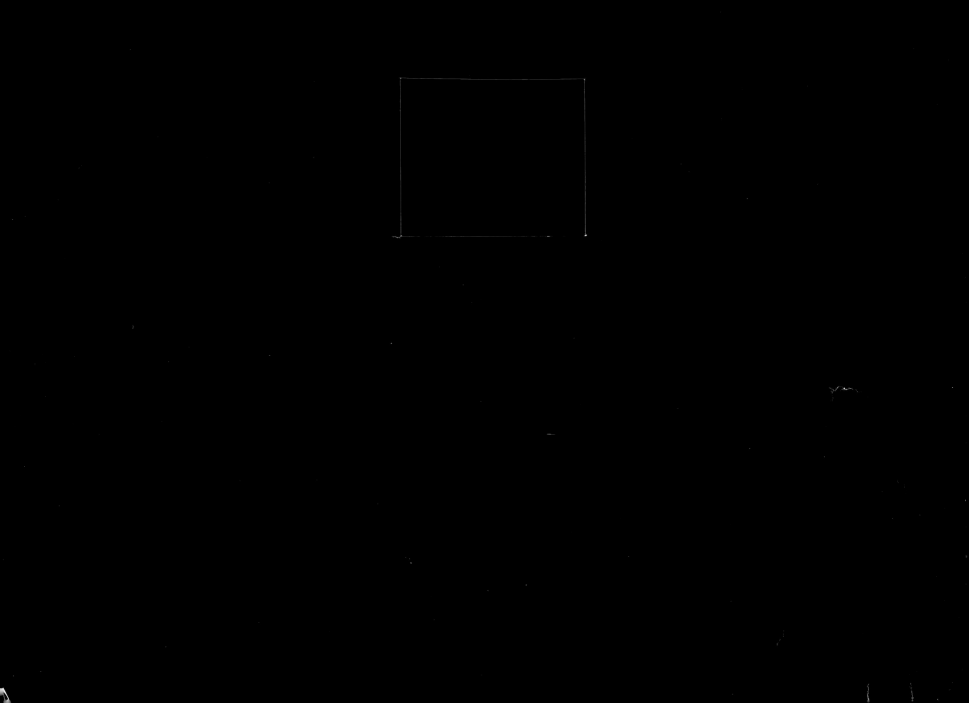

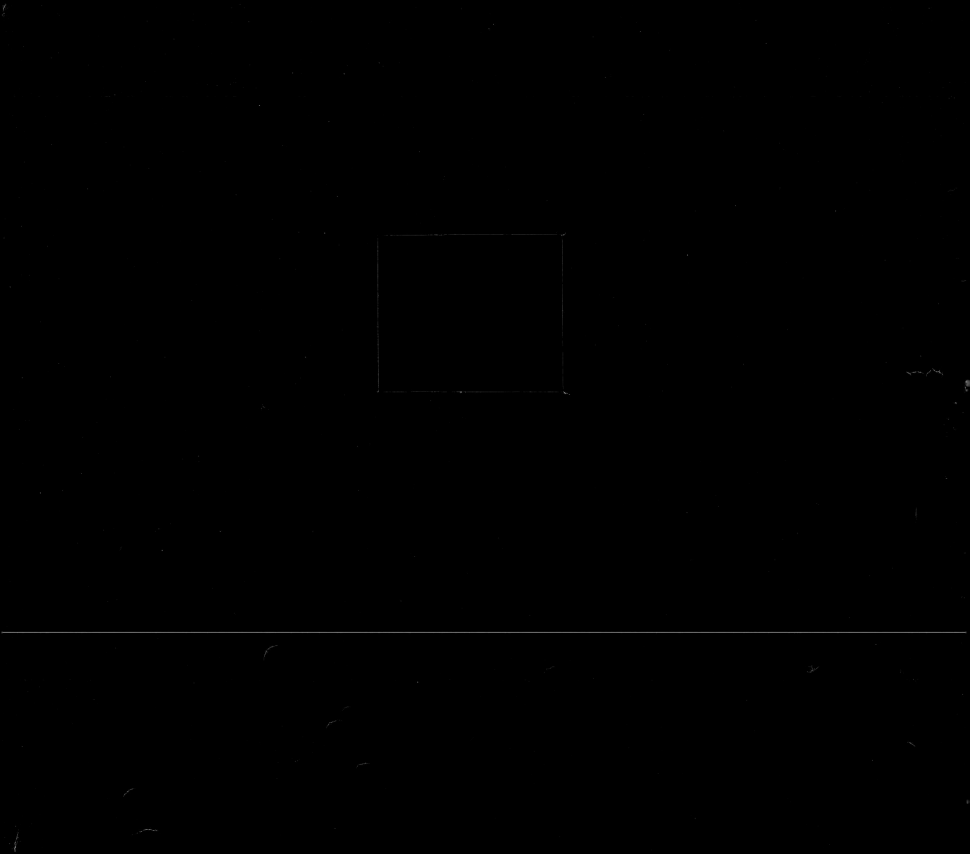